THE PUPPY PLACE

MUTTLEY

THE PUPPY PLACE

**Don't miss any of these
other stories by Ellen Miles!**

THE PUPPY PLACE

MUTTLEY

ELLEN MILES

LITTLE APPLE

SCHOLASTIC INC.

New York   Toronto   London   Auckland
Sydney   Mexico City   New Delhi   Hong Kong

ISBN 978-0-545-25394-9

Cover art by Tim O'Brien
Original cover design by Steve Scott

12 11 10 9 8 7 6 5 4 3 2 1   10 11 12 13 14 15/0

Printed in the U.S.A.   40

First printing, September 2010

For Barley, of course

CHAPTER ONE

"This way, everybody!" Lizzie Peterson waved a hand, feeling like a real tour guide. She enjoyed showing people around the animal shelter where she volunteered. Lizzie had been helping out at Caring Paws, a place for dogs and cats who needed homes, for over a year. She loved the work, because she loved animals — especially dogs. Her usual day was Saturday, when she would spend all afternoon walking dogs, cleaning kitty-litter boxes, and doing whatever else Ms. Dobbins, the shelter's director, asked her to do.

Lizzie worked hard, but there was always more work to do at the shelter. That was why Lizzie had started the Caring Club, for people who wanted to help animals.

Lizzie's best friend, Maria, had joined the club right away, and she had recently become a shelter volunteer, too. Now Daphne and Brianna, who were both in Lizzie's class at school, wanted to join the club. That was why Lizzie was showing them around the shelter.

Daphne and Brianna had a lot to learn if they were going to become shelter volunteers. Ms. Dobbins would be their official trainer, but she had asked Lizzie to give them a tour on their first visit. Lizzie had spent so much time at Caring Paws that she knew every inch of the place by heart. It was fun to give a tour, especially because Maria had come along, too.

"And this is the cat room," Lizzie said now, as she stopped in front of a big picture window.

"Duh," said Daphne. She nudged Brianna. Brianna giggled. "Like I couldn't have figured that out for myself," Daphne added in a whisper.

Lizzie glared at Daphne. Okay, so maybe it was kind of obvious. They were standing in a hallway of an animal shelter, looking through a window at a roomful of cats: black cats and orange cats, long-haired cats and skinny cats, fat cats and six-toed cats, scampering kittens and calm mama cats, and one big old gray tomcat named Tommy, who always claimed the top lounging shelf. So yes, the room was crawling with cats. Anyone could see that it must be the cat room. But Lizzie was just trying to give a tour, the way Ms. Dobbins had asked. Daphne was not exactly Lizzie's favorite person, but Lizzie knew that the shelter needed all the help it could get.

Lizzie was happy to have more Caring Club members, since the club was pretty small so far. Lizzie's younger brother Charles was a member, and so was their mom. Their dad was too busy as a firefighter, and the Bean, Lizzie's other brother (whose real name was Adam), was too little.

All the Petersons loved animals. They loved them so much that they had become a foster family for puppies. That meant they took care of puppies who needed homes, just until they found each one the perfect forever family.

The Petersons had lots of experience with all kinds of puppies. But the puppy they loved best was Buddy, a little brown-and-white dog. Buddy had started out as a foster puppy but he ended up becoming part of the Peterson family. Lizzie had first met Buddy when he arrived at Caring Paws along with his mother and two other puppies.

Now, at the shelter, Lizzie smiled. Just the thought of Buddy made her heart melt. Had there ever been a cuter, sweeter puppy? She loved to stroke the heart-shaped white patch on his chest and whisper secrets into his silky ears.

"Lizzie." Maria stuck an elbow into Lizzie's side. "Weren't you showing Daphne and Brianna the cat room?"

Oops. Lizzie blinked. *Right.* She was in the middle of showing her classmates around. "Yes," she said. "So, the cat room. Lots to do in there, like cleaning out litter boxes, making sure the water dishes are full of clean water, and helping out at feeding time. And sometimes I help hold the cats when the vet is giving them shots."

"My cat Jenny scratches when she's at the vet," said Daphne, "but —"

"If you wrap them up in a towel, that usually helps," Lizzie said. "They can't scratch you then." She led her group down the hall, toward the dog room. "Ready to meet the dogs?"

Behind her, she heard Daphne whisper to Brianna, "That's just what I was about to say. We always wrap Jenny in a towel."

Lizzie knew she should probably be glad that Daphne knew a few things about caring for animals. But she was the one giving the tour, wasn't she? Maybe Daphne should do more listening and less talking.

"Do I hear Greta barking?" Maria asked. "She must be ready for her walk."

"Yeah, that's Greta, all right," said Lizzie. "She knows it's time to go out."

"I'll walk her," said Daphne. "Where's her leash?"

"Well, Greta can be a handful," Lizzie began. "She's —"

"I can handle a handful," Daphne said. "Just show me to her cage."

"We call them kennels," Lizzie said as she pushed open the door to the dog room. "And Greta's in number one." She had to shout to be heard over the barking that had started the second they'd entered the dog room. All the dogs loved to greet new visitors. Lizzie pointed to the hand-painted NUMBER ONE sign on the very first kennel they came to. A special heavy-weight leash hung from the clip on the door.

Daphne looked into Greta's kennel. Then she looked at Lizzie.

Lizzie smiled. "Still want to take her for a walk?" she asked.

Greta was the biggest dog ever to stay at

Caring Paws. She was a bullmastiff, with a tawny golden brown coat and black markings on her huge, sweet, drooly face. Greta was gigantic. If Greta stood on her hind legs, she would be taller than Lizzie. She would probably be taller than Lizzie's dad.

Lizzie saw Daphne gulp.

Then Daphne shrugged. "Sure," she said. "Why not?"

Lizzie shrugged, too. "Okay, then," she said. Daphne could find out for herself how hard it could be to handle Greta. Lizzie checked that the main door to the dog room was closed. "Open her kennel door just enough to get the leash clipped on. Then take her down the aisle and out that way." She pointed to the door that opened into the outside pen.

Daphne squared her shoulders and took a deep breath. Then she unhooked the leash and flipped up the latch on Greta's kennel. Slipping a hand inside, she clipped the leash onto Greta's collar. Then she looked up at Lizzie and grinned. "No problem," she said.

"Open the door slowly!" Lizzie warned. Then she watched as Greta shoved her way out of the kennel and dragged Daphne down the aisle, barreling along like an airplane speeding down a runway.

"Aaaaah!" yelled Daphne as she dashed along after Greta, hanging on for dear life.

Lizzie held back a laugh and looked at Maria. Maria shook her head at Lizzie. Lizzie knew what Maria was thinking. Lizzie probably should have told Daphne that Greta did not know how to walk on a leash without pulling with the strength of an ox.

Ten minutes later, as Lizzie was showing Brianna how to wash out the dogs' water bowls, Greta towed Daphne back inside. The knees of Daphne's jeans were covered in mud, her jacket sleeve was torn, and her hair was tousled and tangled.

"Isn't Greta terrific?" Lizzie asked as she opened the big dog's kennel door for Daphne.

"Terrific," said Daphne. "Just terrific." She brushed the mud from her knees. "Who's next?"

Hmmm. Lizzie realized that Daphne was not going to admit that Greta had been too much for her. Well, she had another challenge for her, then. It was important to make sure that the new volunteers could handle anything. "A much quieter dog," she said. "A puppy, actually. His name is Muttley."

CHAPTER TWO

While Maria helped Brianna get another dog ready for a walk, Lizzie led Daphne down to kennel number four.

"This is Muttley," she said. Inside the kennel, a tan-and-brown puppy lay curled up on his green bed. He had floppy ears, a black nose, and cute, brown eyebrow-shaped markings above his eyes.

"He's cute," said Daphne. "Hi, Muttley."

Muttley opened one brown eye to look at Daphne. Then he sighed, stretched out his legs, and went back to sleep.

"What breed is he?" asked Daphne.

"He's a mix," said Lizzie. "He's part German shepherd and part Walker hound. I knew it the second I saw him." Lizzie had practically memo-rized the "Dog Breeds of the World" poster on her bedroom wall. "He's only about six months old. He'll be a medium-sized dog when he grows up."

"Hey, cutie," said Daphne.

Muttley's eyebrows twitched, but he did not wake up.

Muttley loved to sleep. Every single time Lizzie came to the shelter, Muttley was asleep. He did not jump up like the other dogs. He did not put his paws on the wire door of his kennel and beg for treats. He did not play with any of the toys in his kennel. He just lay on his green bed, snoozing. He wasn't a sad dog; his tail would thump on the floor when any-body came by, and he was always happy to see Lizzie. He just liked to sleep. Sometimes he snored a little. Once in a great while, he would sit up, look around, and let out a deep, hoarse bark that trailed off into the low, mournful *aaaoooooowww* of a hound howl. Then he would circle his bed three or four times and settle back in for a nap.

"He's not very lively, is he?" Daphne stared into Muttley's kennel.

Lizzie shook her head.

"Is something wrong with him?" Daphne asked. "I mean, is he sick?"

Lizzie shook her head again. "The vet checked him out when he first came. And she looked him over again last week, because we all wondered why he's so sleepy. But she says he's completely healthy."

"How long has he been here?" Daphne bent down and stuck a finger through the wire mesh to scratch Muttley's head. Muttley shifted in his sleep but he did not open his eyes.

"About three weeks," Lizzie said. She felt bad for Muttley. When people came to look for a dog to adopt, they liked to see one who sat up and looked back at them. Nobody liked the dogs who jumped and barked their heads off, but nobody seemed to like this quiet puppy, either. Lizzie could sort of understand that. What was the point of adopting a puppy who was going to do nothing but sleep, sleep, sleep? "Anyway, want to walk him? He definitely needs to get outside."

"Sure." Daphne unhooked the blue leash from Muttley's kennel door, flipped up the latch, and stepped inside to clip the leash onto his collar. Muttley didn't get up. He rolled over with a groan. "Come on, Muttley," said Daphne. "Don't you want to go for a walk?" She tugged on the leash, and Muttley groaned again and put a paw over his head.

Leave me alone, I'm sleepy.

Lizzie giggled. She could just imagine what Muttley was thinking.

Daphne frowned. "How can I get him going? Maybe if —"

Lizzie interrupted. "Sometimes if you have a treat, he gets interested." She reached into her pocket for one of the mini-biscuits she always carried when she was at the shelter, and handed it to Daphne.

"That's what I was about to say." Daphne tossed her head. "How about a cookie, Muttley?" Daphne said in an encouraging way. "Want a biscuit?" She held it to his nose. Muttley took the biscuit very gently from her hand, crunched it up, and swallowed. Then he sighed, tucked his legs in more comfortably, and settled back in for more napping. Daphne blew a breath up toward her bangs.

"Just pick him up," Lizzie said.

Daphne frowned at Lizzie. "I was going to." She knelt down and pulled the lazy little puppy into her arms.

"Not like that!" Lizzie said. "Hold him underneath his tummy."

Daphne glared. "My cousin is a vet, and she showed me how to hold a puppy. She said this way is fine." But she shifted the puppy in her arms. "Okay, Muttley. I guess I'm going to have to carry you out." Muttley barely opened his eyes as she carried him down the aisle and out the door.

Brianna and Maria were done walking dogs, so while Daphne walked Muttley, Lizzie showed Brianna how to hose down an empty kennel to clean it out and get it ready for the next dog. There was always a "next dog" at the shelter — that was the sad thing. There were so many unwanted pets in the world.

When Daphne came back in, Muttley walked next to her on the leash. He yawned as she let him into his kennel, and he headed straight for his bed.

Phew. Glad that's over. I'm ready for a nap.

All four girls gathered at his kennel to look in on the sleepy pup. "He's really adorable," said Brianna. "I can't believe nobody has adopted him yet."

Ms. Dobbins had just come into the dog room. She joined the girls at Muttley's kennel. "People like to see a puppy with some pep," she said. "I think he's just a little too mellow for most folks. I'm beginning to worry about him. He needs to get into a home soon, while he's young, so he can learn about living with people."

"Why doesn't your family take him?" Daphne asked Lizzie. "Don't you foster puppies all the time?"

Lizzie nodded. "We had another puppy with us when Muttley first got here," she said. "And then — I don't know. I guess I just didn't think of it." She looked at Muttley. He really was cute, but he had not exactly captured her heart. Maybe she was like the people Ms. Dobbins talked about — the people who liked puppies with energy and personality. Muttley was so quiet that it was almost easy to forget he was there.

"That's a great idea," said Ms. Dobbins. "I'd hate to see Muttley stay here too much longer. Maybe being in a home — especially a home with a lively puppy like Buddy — would help get him energized enough that someone will want to adopt him permanently."

"Maybe," said Lizzie. "But I'd have to ask my parents. It might not be a good time. My mom's away. She drove down to North Carolina to visit her sister." She felt a pang as she spoke. She had been so busy at the shelter that she had nearly forgotten that Mom would not be there when she got home. Mom had left the day before, Monday, and she wouldn't be back until the *next* Monday. A week was a long time. But Mom's sister, Lizzie's aunt Julie, had just had a big operation. She needed Mom's help.

Lizzie nearly forgot about Muttley until it was time to go. There was so much to show the others and to explain about dogs and their behavior. But when Dad came to pick Lizzie and Maria up, Ms. Dobbins told him about Muttley. Dad came back to the dog room to check him out.

"Hey there, pal." Dad looked into the kennel.

Muttley opened one eye and looked up at Dad. He thumped his tail.

"He doesn't look like much of a troublemaker. I think we can handle him, even with Mom away. I bet we can find this boy a home before she even gets back. We'd be happy to take him. Right, Lizzie?"

Lizzie looked at Muttley. He wasn't the most exciting puppy in the world, but he sure was adorable. Plus Lizzie reminded herself about Bear, a husky her family had fostered. He had seemed sleepy and lazy at first, too. But Lizzie had fallen in love with him, just as she fell in love with every puppy her family fostered. Why should Muttley be the exception? "Right," she said.

CHAPTER THREE

At lunchtime at school the next day, Maria asked Lizzie how Muttley was doing.

"He's fine, I guess." Lizzie licked the lid she had just peeled off her applesauce. She liked to eat her dessert first at lunch. "All he does is sleep, sleep, sleep. I've been calling him Sleepy, because he reminds me of the dwarf in 'Snow White.' You know, the one who can barely keep his eyes open?"

Maria laughed. "What does Buddy think?"

"Buddy's confused," said Lizzie. "He loves to play with other puppies, but Muttley doesn't want to play much." She finished her applesauce and unwrapped her sandwich. Turkey on whole wheat?

Didn't Dad know she hated turkey sandwiches? Mom never gave her turkey.

"There must be something to love about Muttley." Maria held up her sandwich — tuna on pita bread — with a questioning glance. Lizzie nodded, and the girls traded.

"Well, he is incredibly cute. And Dad thinks he's actually really smart," Lizzie said. "He can tell by the way Muttley makes eye contact when you talk to him. That means he looks you right in the eye. At least when he's awake, that is," she added. "That's the German shepherd in him, I bet."

She took a bite of sandwich. "Anyway, Dad thinks it will be easy to find a home for Muttley. I hope he's right. My mom wasn't that happy to hear that we agreed to take a foster puppy while she was gone. She said she was ready for a break from fostering for a while, and hoping to come back to a one-puppy household. We had to promise to find Muttley a home before she gets back."

Lizzie looked up and saw Daphne and Brianna on their way out of the hot-lunch line. They carried their trays to the table and sat down across from Lizzie and Maria.

Lizzie did her best not to make a face when she saw the gross shepherd's pie on their plates. She would rather have a turkey sandwich anytime. "So, when are you coming to Caring Paws again?"

Daphne and Brianna looked at each other. "Actually, we can't make it anytime soon," said Daphne.

"Um, right," said Brianna. "We're both kind of busy."

"Maybe you shouldn't count on us for help at the shelter," Daphne said.

"Yeah, I'm not sure I have time to be in the Caring Club, either," added Brianna.

"What do you mean? Why not?" asked Lizzie. Neither girl answered. Lizzie looked at Maria. Maria didn't look back at her. At that moment, Maria seemed very interested in her sandwich.

"Well, fine." Lizzie turned back to Daphne and Brianna. "Whatever. If you don't want to be in the Caring Club and help animals, I won't force you. There are plenty of other kids who want to join." She didn't mention that most of the other kids were little, Charles's friends. So what? Even little kids could help animals.

"I'll come. I heard about your club. I want to be in the Caring Club."

Lizzie looked up to see who was talking. *Oh, no.* "Hi, Jimmy," she said. "Um, right now the club is kind of full."

"But I love animals!" Jimmy squeezed his way onto the bench next to Brianna, knocking a half-full carton of chocolate milk off her tray.

"Oops," said Jimmy. "Sorry! Sorry, Brianna. I'm really sorry." He jumped up to grab a bunch of paper towels, then smeared the chocolate milk all over the table and the floor.

This was exactly why Lizzie didn't want Jimmy Johnston to be in the club. It was bad enough to have him in her class, where he was always distracting everyone. He talked all the time and jumped up and knocked things over. Even when he sat still, he had to jiggle something: his leg would move like the needle of a sewing machine, or a pencil in his hand would *tap-tap-tap* on the desk. Some days it seemed as if Mrs. Abeson said nothing all day but "Jimmy, settle down. Jimmy, it's someone else's turn to talk. Jimmy, that's not classroom behavior."

Lizzie knew that Jimmy didn't *mean* to be the way he was. "Maybe there's another club you could join," she said.

"But I'm really good with dogs. My gramps calls me —" Jimmy began, but just then the bell rang and it was time to line up and head back to class.

"Maybe you shouldn't say no to him so fast," Maria whispered to Lizzie as they tossed their sandwich scraps into the composting bin.

"Are you kidding?" Lizzie whispered back. "He'd make the animals nuts with all that energy."

Maria shrugged. "Maybe," she said as she balled up her lunch bag and tossed it into the trash. "But I bet Ms. Dobbins wouldn't mind the extra help. And if Daphne and Brianna aren't going to be in the Caring Club, then you might wish you had some other members."

"Oh, they'll come back," Lizzie said as she and Maria took their places in line behind Mrs. Abeson, by the cafeteria doors.

"I wouldn't be so sure about that," Maria said.

Lizzie looked at her. "Why?"

Maria was busy looking at her sneakers.

"Maria, why don't they want to be in the club? Do you know something I don't know?" Lizzie stared at her friend until Maria finally met her eyes.

"They think . . . well, I heard that Daphne said you're a bossy know-it-all," said Maria quickly, and very quietly. Then she looked back down at her sneakers.

"Bossy? Me?"

Mrs. Abeson waved. "Let's go, kiddos," she called. She walked out of the cafeteria, leading her class down the hall and up the stairs back to their room. But Lizzie stood still, with her hands on her hips. It was almost funny that Daphne had said that. Daphne Drake was the one who was a know-it-all. She was the biggest know-it-all in fourth grade. "Come on, you've got to be kidding. All I did was show them around the shelter."

Maria shrugged. "I guess it wasn't so much what you did as how you did it. You can't help it, really. You do know an awful lot about the shelter, and about animals, and about the best ways to take care of them." She tugged Lizzie's sleeve. "Come on." Maria pulled Lizzie down the hall, following Mrs. Abeson and the rest of their class.

"Right, and I was trying to share what I know. What's so wrong with that?" Lizzie shook her head. Some people just didn't get it.

"Nothing," said Maria as they walked into their classroom. "Just . . . maybe there are better and worse ways to share."

CHAPTER FOUR

"Woolly Bully!" Lizzie yelled as she tossed a raggedy grayish stuffed sheep to Charles.

Charles caught the sheep and ran toward the stairs, then spun around and threw the toy back to Lizzie. "Woolly Bully!" he cried.

Buddy dashed back and forth between them, scrabbling and skidding on the floor as he tried to make a quick turn to grab the flying sheep out of the air. His ears were on full alert, his eyes were bright, and he barked and wagged his tail in crazy circles. Buddy loved to play Woolly Bully.

So did Lizzie — especially when it took her mind off other things, like . . . well, what had happened at school that day. Who cared what Daphne Drake thought? But Lizzie felt her stomach clench up every time she remembered what Daphne had said. She wished she could talk to Mom about it, but Mom wasn't there. "Woolly Bully, Woolly Bully, Woolly Bully!" she chanted as she held the sheep high above Buddy's head.

Lizzie couldn't remember exactly how or when this game had been invented, but she knew that "Wooly Bully" was an old song her dad liked. He was the one who had named the stuffed sheep and taught them the song. Sort of. He didn't exactly know the words, just the part where you sang "Wooly Bully" over and over again. Charles and Lizzie and Buddy had made up the rest of the game, which was a combination of catch, touch football, keep-away, and monkey in the middle.

Mom wasn't crazy about Woolly Bully. "Too wild for indoors," she always said.

But Mom was away, and Dad didn't mind if Lizzie and Charles played Woolly Bully. He was all for it if it might get Muttley moving. "We've got to rev that dog up if we want to find him a home," he'd said. And the game had worked — for a little while. Muttley had joined right in, chasing the toy sheep as it flew from hand to hand. But now — Lizzie paused, holding the sheep — where was that sleepyhead?

Buddy jumped up and grabbed the sheep out of Lizzie's hand. Then he ran straight into the living room and did three laps around the couch, shaking the sheep happily.

Wheee! Got it.

For the first time since lunch, Lizzie laughed. That was the great thing about dogs. They made you laugh, even when you felt awful. She went to look for Muttley. "What are you doing up here?" she asked the puppy when she found him asleep in the upstairs hall, just outside the Bean's room.

She sat down next to him and stroked his floppy ears. Muttley stretched out his legs and sighed happily.

Aaah, that feels good.

"That seems to be his favorite spot lately," said Dad, coming up the stairs. "I noticed that he came up to check on the Bean yesterday at naptime. Then he slept outside the door, as if he was guarding him. I guess he's just in the habit now, even though the Bean is at day care today."

"That's sweet," said Lizzie. "What a good boy. He's a sleepy little hound, but he also likes to take care of his people, like a shepherd." Lizzie remembered how impressed Ms. Dobbins had been when Lizzie had guessed Muttley's mix of breeds. It had been easy. Lizzie had recognized Muttley's long ears and face markings from the Walker hound picture on her poster, and his brown-and-tan coloring and long wavy tail were all shepherd. Ms. Dobbins didn't think Lizzie was a know-it-all. Or did she?

Lizzie pulled the sleepy, warm Muttley onto her lap and kissed the soft black fur on his nose. She remembered the day before at the shelter, when she had shown Brianna the best way to clean a dog dish. She had taken the dish out of Brianna's hands and scrubbed it herself, explaining that you had to use the hottest water and plenty of soap, and then make sure to rinse it really well.

Hmmm. Maybe Brianna would have figured that out on her own.

Thinking about it, Lizzie could understand how that might have *seemed* like something a bossy person would do.

Then she remembered how she had interrupted Daphne when Daphne was trying to share her own ideas about caring for animals, and how she'd corrected the way Daphne picked Muttley up. Was that being a know-it-all? "What do you think, Muttley?" Lizzie asked.

Muttley opened one eye and licked Lizzie's hand.

I think I like the way you're petting me.

Lizzie wondered what it would take to get Daphne and Brianna to give her — and the shelter — another chance.

Later, while Lizzie helped her dad get dinner ready, she asked, "Dad, do you think I'm bossy? Or, like, a know-it-all?"

Dad smiled as he stirred a big pot of chili, which filled the kitchen with delicious smells. Dad had learned to cook way back when he was a rookie firefighter, living at the firehouse. Firefighters had big appetites, and they liked hearty meals. Dad's specialties were blueberry pancakes and chili. Actually, now that Lizzie thought of it, she realized that those were pretty much the only two things he ever made.

"Well," he said, "you do have a . . . a kind of strong personality at times."

"What he means," said Charles, who had just come in to grab some pretzels for himself and some dog biscuits for Buddy and Muttley, "is yes, you're bossy." He crossed his eyes at Lizzie. "Definitely very, very bossy."

"That's enough of that, pal." Dad turned back to Lizzie. "No, all I meant was that you do know a lot about certain topics — like dogs, for instance — and you're not shy about saying what you think. Some people might call that being bossy or a know-it-all. I call it Lizzie." He swooped her into a big hug. "You're my girl," he whispered into her ear, "and your mom and I will always be proud of you."

CHAPTER FIVE

Mom called just as they finished dinner. After Charles had given her the Muttley Report (still sleepy, no forever home yet), and Mom had given everyone the Aunt Julie Update (feeling much better, still having a hard time getting around), Lizzie took over the phone and told Mom what had happened that day. "That dumb Daphne Drake said I was a bossy know-it-all," she said.

"That wasn't very nice," said Mom. "But maybe she didn't mean it the way it came out. Maybe Daphne is just a little envious of how much you know about animals."

"I never thought of that," said Lizzie. "But, Mom, do you think I'm bossy sometimes?"

For a second, Mom didn't say anything.

"Mom?" asked Lizzie.

"Sometimes, yes," Mom finally said. "You do have a way of ordering people around — your brothers, for example. But you are also a kind, loving big sister, and they are lucky to have you."

Now Lizzie was silent for a moment. "I miss you, Mom," she said finally. She sniffed and wiped her eyes as she said good-bye.

"How about a special treat?" Dad asked after Lizzie had hung up. "How about Movie Night?"

"Really? Even though it's a weeknight?" Lizzie asked. Usually Movie Night was a weekend thing. She had a feeling Dad knew how sad she felt saying good-bye to Mom.

"Why not?" Dad asked. "It's still early, so you probably won't even be up past your bedtimes. Not much, anyway. Not enough to tell Mom." He held a finger to his lips. "It'll be our secret."

"Yayyy!" they all yelled. Charles and Lizzie and the Bean loved to pile into the big bed in Mom and Dad's room to watch a movie.

"Can we bring our ice cream?" asked Charles. That was another special treat: Dad had brought home vanilla-chocolate-strawberry ice cream *and* chocolate sauce.

"Hmmm," Dad said. "That might be a mistake."

Lizzie pictured it: the Bean + ice cream + chocolate sauce + bed = yikes! Mom would not be happy to come back to that kind of mess. She nodded. "We'll have ice cream down here, before the movie," she said. They took their bowls into the living room and Lizzie got the Bean settled at the coffee table, with lots of paper towels on hand to wipe up any messes. She sat on the floor nearby and pulled Muttley into her lap for a cuddle. Muttley rested his head on her knee and let out a contented sigh.

There are so many nice spots for napping here. I like this place.

Lizzie patted his soft ears between bites of ice cream. She always tried to make her chocolate and strawberry (she never bothered with vanilla) come out even.

Charles and the Bean played tug with Buddy while they ate their ice cream. Buddy was always ready for a game. He *grrr*ed and yipped and pulled at Mr. Duck (his favorite toy) while Charles hung on. When Charles let him win the game, he ran off with Mr. Duck to another corner of the room, hoping someone would chase him. Then he pranced back to Charles, waving Mr. Duck in his face until Charles started the tug game over. The Bean's main job in the game was to laugh and shriek and yell, "Buddy, come! Buddy, give toy!" and laugh some more until he sat down with a bump. After a moment of silence, his laughter would start all over again.

"Which movie should we watch?" Charles asked. He fanned out the three movies Dad had brought home.

"Dis one." The Bean grabbed at one about a purple stuffed rabbit.

Charles and Lizzie groaned. "That's for babies," said Lizzie.

"How about this one?" Charles held up a movie about robots that come to life.

Lizzie waved it away. "Dumb. This one." She picked up the last movie. "This is the one we'll watch. It'll be great."

Charles started to say something, but then he shrugged. "No wonder," he said under his breath.

Lizzie frowned at him. "What did you say? No wonder *what*?"

"No wonder Daphne thinks you're bossy." Charles looked down at the DVD in his hand. "I hate to tell you," he went on, "but Sammy and David kind of agree with Daphne. They've seen you in action before, and they don't want to be bossed around, either. So they, um, they changed their minds about helping out at Caring Paws."

Lizzie shook her head. What was there to say? No Daphne and Brianna. No Sammy or

David. Was Jimmy Johnston the only person left who wanted to join the Caring Club? She got up and headed for the stairs. "Let's just watch the movie."

The movie was about a boy who lived in Alaska, where he and his team of huskies entered a sled-dog race. Lizzie knew it would be exciting. She could still hardly believe that she had once gotten to drive a dogsled herself. It was the most incredible thing she had ever done.

Even when she was upset — maybe *especially* when she was upset — Lizzie loved to snuggle into Mom and Dad's bed, with its soft pillows and its heavy, warm spread and its sweet, safe, sleepy smell. The Bean cuddled up right next to her, and Charles and Buddy lay across the bottom of the bed in their favorite spot. Dad got the movie going, then headed downstairs to check on Muttley and clean up the kitchen.

The movie was just as exciting as Lizzie had imagined. She forgot all about what Charles had told her — and even about what Daphne had said — as she watched the beautiful barking dogs pull a sled through the snowy scenery. But somehow — maybe because she was so cozy — she kept drifting off to sleep, only to wake with a start, realizing she had missed a whole section of the story.

She was snoozing again when she was woken by the sound of barking — from downstairs. It didn't come from the movie. It was a hoarse bark, followed by a long, howling *aaaooooowww*. Muttley!

The barking came closer, joined by the pounding of footsteps up the stairs. "Here they are, Muttley," Dad said as he pushed open the bedroom door. "They're safe and sound, see?"

Muttley leapt onto the bed and licked each of their faces in turn: first Charles's, then the Bean's, and finally Lizzie's. Then he curled up between Lizzie and the Bean and, with a sigh, settled right into a deep sleep.

My work is done. Time for a nap.

Lizzie stroked Muttley's head. "What's going on?" she asked.

Dad shook his head. "I'm telling you, this is one smart pooch," he said. "Last I saw, he was asleep in the living room. But he must have slipped upstairs to check on each of you in your beds — and when he didn't find you, he came galloping back down, barking his head off to let me know you were missing."

"He forgot to look in here," said Charles.

"Why would he? He's already learned where each of you usually sleeps. But I bet he'll never miss checking this bedroom again," said Dad. He sat on the bed and patted Muttley. "This pup is going to grow up into a great dog. We've got to get the word out on him. Someone will want a smart pup like this."

Muttley looked up at Dad and gave a huge pink-tongue-rolling yawn.

Are you ever *going to stop talking, so I can get* *back to sleep?*

Lizzie laughed. "Oh, Muttley." She gave him a big hug and kissed his nose. He really was a sweetie. "Thanks for taking care of us."

CHAPTER SIX

By Friday morning, Lizzie was a little tired of hearing Dad talk about how smart Muttley was. She had started to put her hands over Buddy's ears so he wouldn't hear and get his feelings hurt. So what if (as Dad sometimes said) Buddy wasn't exactly the smartest cookie in the box? He was no dummy. Lizzie had taught Buddy how to do at least seven tricks, including shake hands, give a high five, and roll over.

Lizzie was also tired of a few other things. For one, chili. Dad's chili was good, but did he have to make such a huge pot of it? The leftovers seemed never to end. They had eaten chili for dinner on Tuesday night, Wednesday night, and Thursday night. Three nights in a row, and there was still some in the pot. Even with ice cream for dessert, that was a little too much chili. Lizzie thought longingly of Mom's cheesy lasagna, and delicious baked pork chops, and spicy Mexican casserole. Even pizza would be a good change. Even *frozen* pizza.

Speaking of Mom, Lizzie was tired of her being away. She missed her mother — and not only because of lasagna. Even though Mom had called twice the day before and listened while Lizzie told her all about Muttley, it wasn't the same as having her there. Lizzie wished Mom were coming home that weekend instead of on Monday.

Lizzie was tired of worrying about how to get volunteers to come to Caring Paws. It had not been easy to tell Ms. Dobbins that Charles's friends wouldn't be coming after all. To make up for that, Lizzie had spent an extra two hours helping out at the shelter on Thursday afternoon, and had promised to keep coming every day after school and extra on Saturday.

And she was very, *very* tired of Daphne. At school, when Lizzie spoke about Muttley at morning meeting, Daphne kept whispering to Brianna.

"Daphne, please show respect for Lizzie when she's talking," Mrs. Abeson had to say about three times.

"But Lizzie has talked about Muttley every day this week," Daphne said. "It's getting boring."

Lizzie rolled her eyes. She might be bossy, but at least she wasn't rude.

Now morning meeting was over. It was free-reading time and Lizzie could not find her book, *Understood Betsy*. She loved that book so much that she was reading it for the second time. It was a cozy, old-fashioned story about a girl who went to stay with her relatives in Vermont.

Lizzie pawed through her desk. She looked underneath her spelling workbook and checked inside her math folder. Where was that book? All the other kids were already settled into their favorite spots, reading.

Then Lizzie remembered that she had taken her book home the day before. Maybe it was still in her backpack, which was in her cubby. Lizzie sighed, got up, and went behind the big bookcase in the back of the classroom to look.

Aha! There it was. Lizzie pulled the book out of her backpack. If she was lucky, she'd still have a few minutes to read. Then she heard a sniff. She turned and saw a small figure sitting very, very still, tucked inside a cubby in the farthest corner. "Jimmy?" she asked. "Is that you?" Jimmy *never* sat that still. But she recognized his blue plaid shirt and the floppy brown hair that hid his eyes. She took a step closer, unsure.

It *was* Jimmy. He sat quietly with his arms wrapped around his knees.

"What's the matter?" Lizzie went to sit beside the cubby.

He sniffed again and wiped his nose with his shirtsleeve. "I just — I just want a dog so bad," he said.

That was a surprise.

"A dog?" Lizzie asked.

He nodded. "You're so lucky. You have your own puppy and you get to foster puppies, too."

Lizzie knew that Jimmy was right. She *was* lucky. She remembered wanting a dog so bad — so bad she could have cried.

"Muttley sounds like such a cool dog," Jimmy said. "Smart, too."

Lizzie nodded. Now she understood. Hearing her talk about Muttley had made Jimmy sad. "He is," she said. Then she had a great idea. "Maybe your family could adopt him."

Jimmy shook his head. "I keep asking and asking if I can get a dog. I would take care of it, and walk it, and feed it, and everything. My parents are divorced, and Mom just says no way. She's not a dog person. Dad says he'd love to have a dog but he works funny hours sometimes and he'd hate to leave the dog home alone."

Lizzie knew exactly how Jimmy felt — because

it was exactly how *she* had felt for a very long time. She had wanted a dog for years and years before she finally got Buddy. Poor Jimmy. Then she sat up straight and smiled. She'd just had another great idea. "Hey, Jimmy," she said. "Remember how you said you wanted to join the Caring Club, and help out at the shelter?"

CHAPTER SEVEN

"Welcome, Jimmy," said Ms. Dobbins that afternoon, when Lizzie and Jimmy arrived at Caring Paws. "We are full to overflowing here these days, with lots of dogs and cats who need homes. We can use all the help we can get." She barely stopped to smile at Jimmy and Lizzie as she unloaded giant bags of dog food from a truck. "For today, just do whatever Lizzie tells you to do. She knows the routine."

Jimmy turned to Lizzie and gave her a salute. "At your service!" he said.

It was funny: now that she pretty much had permission to act bossy, Lizzie didn't feel as if she needed to. After she'd given Jimmy a quick tour of the shelter, she suggested, "How about if we start by cleaning out the kitty-litter boxes? That's the worst job of all, so I like to get it over with first."

"Okay," said Jimmy. "I've helped change my baby cousin's diapers. That's probably even worse. P.U.!" He held his nose and smiled at Lizzie.

Lizzie smiled back. Jimmy was definitely in a better mood now that he was at the shelter. And he wasn't being too annoying. Actually, he wasn't being annoying at all. Maybe he was only that way when he had to sit still, like in school. She led him into the cat room and showed him what to do. Jimmy didn't make faces or say, "Ew," the way Daphne probably would have. He just got to work.

When they were done, Lizzie and Jimmy took a moment to pay attention to the cats. Ms. Dobbins always said it was important to get them used to being around people. The kittens seemed to love Jimmy, and climbed all over his shoulders to lick his ears. The mama cats sat nearby to keep a watchful eye on their kittens as Jimmy petted each one, holding them as gently as if they were fine china. Even Tommy, the old gray tomcat, slunk down from his high perch and wrapped himself around Jimmy's legs, purring loudly.

Lizzie stared. She had never seen Tommy do *that* before.

Next it was time to walk dogs. "I love taking the dogs out. It's my absolute favorite chore here," Lizzie told Jimmy as she opened the door to the dog room.

Jimmy's eyes brightened when he heard the dogs start to bark. He laughed. "They're happy to see us." He had to yell to be heard over the racket. He began to walk up and down the aisles between the kennels, stopping at each kennel door to look at the dog inside.

Lizzie noticed something. All the dogs went on barking — except for whichever one Jimmy happened to be looking at. That dog — at the moment it was Fluffy, a little Pekingese — sat quietly and looked back at Jimmy with big, curious eyes. It was as if the dogs were waiting with interest to hear what Jimmy had to say.

And Jimmy was saying things to them. Things that Lizzie couldn't quite hear. He spoke very quietly and gave each dog his full attention. He held his hands up to the kennel doors so that the dogs could sniff him.

Jimmy stood very still at each kennel. He was almost as still, Lizzie thought, as he had been when she had found him sitting inside his cubby.

"You're really good with animals," she said to him.

He nodded. "That's what I was trying to tell you the other day. My gramps calls me the Dog Whisperer. He says I'm the only one his old basset hound, Sadie, ever listens to. She's very stubborn, but I can get her to do anything."

"Cool," said Lizzie. Jimmy really did deserve a dog of his own. But if he couldn't have that, at least he could be around these dogs, here at Caring Paws. "Ready to walk some dogs?" she asked.

Jimmy nodded eagerly.

Lizzie started him off with the easiest dog: an old, slow black Lab named Casey, who liked to mosey around and sniff every single weed in the exercise yard. Jimmy clipped on his leash and said, "Come on, Casey."

Lizzie followed them out into the yard with another Lab, a yellow one named Molly. She watched as Casey trotted along, looking much livelier than usual. After Casey, she had Jimmy walk Ramon, a peppy little Chihuahua, and Popeye, a drooly bulldog. Then she decided he was ready for Greta.

"Careful," she said as she handed over Greta's extra-heavy leash. "Greta is really strong, and

she likes to pull. Open the door slowly, and —"
Lizzie stopped herself. She was being bossy again,
and a know-it-all. Jimmy had been great with all
the other dogs. Maybe she should just wait to see
how he handled Greta. Maybe she could learn to
be a know-a-lot, instead of a know-it-all.

Sure enough, Greta didn't pull one bit when
Jimmy walked her. She sailed out of her kennel
with majestic dignity and strolled down the aisle,
gazing up at Jimmy with a look of total adoration
on her big, jowly face.

"Wow," Lizzie said to herself.

She wondered how Muttley would act around
Jimmy. Dogs seemed to be their best when they
were with him. Maybe Jimmy could work some
special magic with the sleepy puppy. "Hey,
Jimmy," she asked when he and Greta came back
in, "do you like chili?"

Jimmy did like chili, and when Lizzie called
to ask Dad if she could invite a friend to dinner,

he said it was fine. Lizzie had hoped that there wouldn't be quite enough chili to go around, and that she'd be forced to have a cheese sandwich for dinner, but unfortunately there was plenty. Lizzie made a face at the big pot that sat warming on the back of the stove when she and Jimmy got home.

Lizzie could tell that Jimmy fell in love with Muttley the moment he saw him. "Look at those floppy ears," he said as he sat down on the floor near Muttley's bed.

Muttley opened one eye.

Then he opened the other one.

He thumped his tail.

Hey! Do I know you? I think I want to know you!

He got up, shook himself until his long ears went *flappety-flap*, and climbed right up onto Jimmy's lap to lick Jimmy's chin and nibble on his shirt collar. Just like Jimmy, Muttley seemed to have fallen in love at first sight. From that moment on, Muttley didn't leave Jimmy alone for a second. He followed him everywhere, sat next to his chair while they ate dinner, and brought him toy after toy to throw and play tug with. If Jimmy stopped paying attention for one second, Muttley would sit back and bark that hoarse bark at him, ending with the long, sad *aaaoooooowww!*

By then, Lizzie wasn't surprised. But Charles, the Bean, and Dad couldn't believe their eyes. "What became of our sleepy pup?" asked Dad as he watched Muttley charge through the living room, racing Buddy to see who would be first to fetch a toy Jimmy had thrown.

When Jimmy's mom came to pick him up, Muttley walked him to the door. Jimmy knelt down to give the puppy a big hug, then stood up and turned quickly to go. Only Lizzie saw how sad Jimmy looked as he followed his mom out the door. Muttley's ears drooped as he plodded back to his bed. He was sad, too.

That was when she knew: Muttley and Jimmy belonged together. All she had to do was figure out how to convince his mom of that. And Lizzie knew that if anybody could do it, she could. After all, *her* mom had not been a dog person, either — until they started fostering puppies.

After Jimmy left, Muttley curled up into a tight little ball on his bed, tucked his nose beneath one paw, and went to sleep. He barely even moved when Lizzie gave him a good-night pat. "What's up, Sir Snores-a-Lot?" she asked. "You're not sick, are you?"

Lizzie felt Muttley's nose. It was moist, just like a healthy dog's nose should be. "Muttley?" she asked. He opened his eyes for a second, and she saw that they were clear and bright. When she leaned down to kiss his little black nose, Muttley's breath smelled sweet. All those signs told Lizzie that Muttley was probably fine.

He was just back to his old ways. Muttley, the World's Laziest Dog. She petted him for a while, then gave him one last kiss on the nose. "Guess I don't have to tell *you* to sleep tight, do I?" She shook her head and smiled at the sleepy pup. Then she went off to bed.

CHAPTER EIGHT

Lizzie was having one of her favorite dreams, the one where she was in the land of dogs. Dogs, dogs, dogs. She was like a little boat bobbing in a vast sea of dogs. She could see dogs of every breed milling around, even the rare breeds, like the komondor. Not too many people would have known what a komondor was, but Lizzie recognized it immediately. The big sheepdog had long white hair, a curtain of ropy cords that hung to the ground from his black nose to his droopy tail. He pranced around with the other dogs, his coat swaying back and forth with every move.

All the dogs ran around happily, barking in their wonderful, different voices. Lizzie heard the *yip-yip-yip* of a Chihuahua and the deep, booming bark of a big old chocolate Lab. Only the basenji and the malamutes, breeds that don't bark, sat quietly and waited for Lizzie to come pat them. Lizzie even heard Muttley's hoarse bark, with that special hound song at the tail end: *aaaaooooowww!*

She laughed and held out her arms for hugs and pats. Five dogs charged over and began to climb on her, licking her face and ears. They licked and slobbered and drooled and —

"Ugh." Lizzie woke up with a start to find that it wasn't all a dream. She really *was* being licked. "Muttley, what are you doing?" Lizzie sat straight up in bed and wiped off her face with her pajama sleeve. "Are you crazy? Cut it out." What was going on? Muttley, the laziest dog in the history of the world, suddenly wanted to play — in the middle of the night?

Muttley whined, jumped off the bed, and ran to the door. Then he turned around, ran back, and

60

leapt up onto the bed to lick Lizzie's face some more, whimpering and whining. Again he threw himself off the bed and scrambled across the floor to the door. He looked back at Lizzie. He whined and barked and howled. *Aaaaooooowww!* he yodeled.

By now, Lizzie was awake enough to realize that something must be wrong. She pushed off her covers and grabbed her robe. "What is it, Muttley?"

But as soon as she was out of bed, Muttley disappeared. She heard him running down the hall to the Bean's room, where he started to bark and howl again.

Danger! Danger! Wake up! Wake up!

Lizzie followed Muttley into the hall — and stopped in her tracks when she smelled something strange. She sniffed, and sniffed again. Then, suddenly, she knew what it was. Smoke!

Her heart began to beat wildly. A few minutes earlier she'd been dreaming a happy dog-show dream. Now she was caught in a real-life nightmare. Was her house about to burn down?

"Dad!" she yelled. "Charles! Fire!" As Muttley skidded and scrambled his way down the hall to Charles's room, Lizzie raced to the Bean's room. She found him standing up in his crib, his eyes wide and his cheeks bright pink. "It's okay. I'm here," she told him. She reached in to help her frightened little brother out.

By the time she and the Bean were in the hall again, Dad and Charles were up, too. A sleepy-looking Buddy stood next to Charles.

Dad yelled to be heard over Muttley's barking and howling. "Stairs are safe." He had already run down and back up again to make sure. "Go on down and straight out the front door. I'll be right behind you." He punched numbers into the phone as he shouted and waved them along, and Lizzie could guess what those numbers were: 9-1-1.

Of course the Petersons had a family fire plan. Lizzie knew that no matter how they each got out of the house, the plan was always the same: they were supposed to meet near the old apple tree in the far corner of the front yard. That way, they would know right away if they had all gotten out safely.

Lizzie picked up the Bean. Usually he was almost too heavy for her to lift, but now he felt light as a feather. She grabbed Charles's hand. She glanced back at her room, wishing she had time to save her model-dog collection — but she knew what Dad would have to say about that. "Come on," she said as she started for the stairs. "Buddy, you, too. Muttley, come."

But when she turned around, she could tell that Muttley was waiting until Dad got moving, too. Muttley barked at Dad. He ran around behind him and nipped at his ankles.

Get out! Get out! Get out!

He didn't stop barking until he had herded all four of them out onto the lawn and followed them to their meeting spot under the apple tree. By that time, his bark was hoarser than ever.

Just a few seconds later, Lizzie heard a siren. Muttley lifted his muzzle to the sky and howled along as the siren drew closer. *Aaaaawwwoooo!* he sang out. Buddy began to bark and howl, too. The sound sent a prickle of fear down Lizzie's neck. Was her house really on fire? This definitely was not a dream anymore. This was real. She didn't have to pinch herself to know that.

Then Lizzie saw flashing lights, and the big hook-and-ladder fire truck roared up their street, with the boxy white ambulance behind it. Three pickup trucks with more flashing lights pulled up and parked every which way in front of the house. Another ambulance roared in and screeched to a stop. In seconds, the yard was full of firefighters in full gear: hats, coats, oxygen tanks, and axes. They charged toward the house and ran through the open front door while Chief Olson and two of the EMTs from the ambulances trotted over to check on the Petersons.

"Is everybody out? Everybody okay?" Chief Olson asked.

Dad nodded.

"Any idea where the fire started?"

Dad shook his head. "I smelled smoke, but that's all I know. We got out as fast as we could."

"The most important thing is that you're all safe," said the chief. He wiped his forehead and smiled at Dad. "When we saw your address on the 911 call, we called out everybody — even these guys from Springfield." He waved at the EMTs from the second ambulance. Dad shook hands with them and thanked them for coming.

Then the front door opened and Meg Parker, one of the firefighters, came out onto the porch, holding something in her outstretched arms. Lizzie couldn't quite make out what the rounded shape was.

"Nothing but some extra-well-done chili," called Meg cheerfully. "Must have been left on the stove. Looks like it had just started to burn."

Lizzie heard Dad let out a breath all in one big whoosh. "Chili!" he said. He slapped his forehead.

CHAPTER NINE

"I can't believe I got all of you out here in the middle of the night for a pot of chili," Dad said to Chief Olson.

Lizzie looked at the chief just in time to see him hide a smile. Was he going to make fun of Dad? Lizzie knew how it could be down at the firehouse. The firefighters teased one another all the time. But the chief just shook his head. "Next time try not to overcook it" was all he said. Then his face turned serious. "It could have turned into something much worse. You did the right thing to call us."

"That's right," said Meg. "What woke you up, anyway? I didn't hear an alarm in there. I guess there wasn't enough smoke yet to set one off."

Lizzie looked at Muttley. Then she looked at Dad. Dad had been right about this dog all along. Muttley really was a little smartie. She knelt down to hug him. "He saved us." She kissed his nose. "Muttley barked and licked my face and woke me up."

The chief raised his eyebrows. "Did he, now?"

Meg smiled at Muttley and got down on her knees to pet him. "What a good boy," she said. Muttley stretched and yawned.

Is it almost time to go back to bed?

Meg laughed. "This must be the foster puppy you've been telling us about. Sleepy, but smart, too. You sure were right about him."

Dad nodded. Everybody else gathered around Muttley and started to pet him. One of the EMTs from Springfield looked up at Dad.

"A foster dog?" he asked as he let Muttley lick his face. "You mean you're looking for a home for this guy? My kid's been begging for a dog. Maybe it's time to cave in."

"Nice work, pup," said one of the other fire-fighters.

"He's a hero," said Meg.

Another firefighter smiled down at Muttley. "Do they have any more like him down at the shelter?" he asked. "Maybe I should go check those dogs out."

Lizzie slept late the next day — the whole family did — but she headed over to Caring Paws as soon as she woke up. She could hardly wait to tell Ms. Dobbins about all the excitement in the middle of the night.

"One of the guys was acting as if he might adopt Muttley," Lizzie reported as she finished the story. That was great — but she hoped that somehow she could convince Jimmy's mother to adopt him first. Muttley and Jimmy belonged together, and there were plenty of other dogs at Caring

Paws for the EMT guy to adopt. "And another guy said that if we had any more like Muttley down here, he would come check them out."

Ms. Dobbins wiped away a tear. She could be very emotional about animals. "Every single dog at this shelter has the potential to be a hero," she said. "Whether that means saving a family from a house fire, or just loving someone who needs love. All these dogs ask for is a home."

Lizzie felt tears spring to her own eyes. "Everybody needs to hear about what Muttley did," she said. "Maybe people would come to the shelter if they knew what great dogs we have here, and maybe more dogs would get adopted."

"Exactly." Ms. Dobbins nodded enthusiastically. "We need to spread the word. It's called publicity, and we are long overdue for some good publicity about the shelter."

"We could have an award ceremony for Muttley, like on the steps of the town hall." Lizzie remembered the ceremony last summer for a firefighter named Joey. Joey had rescued some boaters whose canoe had turned over, dumping them into the lake. "Chief Olson could give him a certificate."

Lizzie could see it all now. When Jimmy's mom heard about Muttley's heroic act, she would forget all about not being a dog person and decide to adopt him. Jimmy would get the dog he'd always wanted, and Muttley would be gone by the time Lizzie's mom came home. That EMT guy, and all the other people who had been inspired by the ceremony, would come down to the shelter and adopt the rest of the dogs who needed homes. Everything was going to work out perfectly. "I bet we could do it tomorrow," she finished.

Ms. Dobbins looked surprised.

Oops. "Am I being too bossy?" Lizzie asked.

Ms. Dobbins waved a hand. "Bossy or not, it's a great idea," she said. "And not the first great idea you've had, either." She smiled at Lizzie. "I'll call the chief now. But we'll need an article in tomorrow morning's newspaper to let people know about it. Could your mom write something? She's great with stories like this one. She always makes me cry when she writes about animals."

"My mom's still away," Lizzie reminded Ms. Dobbins.

Ms. Dobbins looked at Lizzie. "What if you wrote it?" she asked. "After all, you were there. You were a witness. I'm sure you could write that story."

"Me?" Lizzie asked.

"I'm going to call Mr. Baker right now," said Ms. Dobbins. "He loves stories like this. And he'll love the idea of you writing it."

Lizzie knew who Mr. Baker was. He was her mom's boss, the editor of the *Littleton News*. She felt her heart thump-thump. Could she really do it?

"I ordered pizza," Dad told Lizzie when he came to get her at the shelter later that day.

"We can swing by and pick it up right now if you want."

"Sure." Lizzie wasn't really listening. She stared out the window of the car, trying to figure out the first sentence of her newspaper story. Mom always said that the first sentence, which she called the lead, had to draw the reader in. Should it begin with the facts? *Muttley, a mixed-breed puppy from the Caring Paws animal shelter, barked loudly to wake the Peterson family when some chili began to burn in their kitchen. . . .* Or maybe it should be more dramatic: *Four people's lives were saved when Muttley, a heroic foster puppy from the Caring Paws animal shelter, woke them from a deep slumber and herded them out of their burning home. . . .*

"Lizzie?" Dad stopped at a stoplight and peered at her. "Did you hear me? I said we can have pizza for supper." He waved a hand in front of her face. "I thought you'd be thrilled, after all that chili."

"Pizza sounds great." Lizzie smiled at her dad, but she was still thinking about her article. At home, she gobbled down two slices before she asked to be excused. Then she headed upstairs and turned on the computer. Mr. Baker had promised Ms. Dobbins that if Lizzie e-mailed him her story by eight o'clock, he would get it into the next morning's paper. What a great surprise it would be for her family if the article was in the paper when they woke up.

Lizzie worked hard on her article — really hard. Muttley snoozed at her feet as she wrote and rewrote, struggling to get all the facts into a short but exciting story. When she finished, she read it over one more time before she sent it. It wasn't bad.

"Maybe I am too bossy sometimes," she said to Muttley. "But there are some good things about me, too. I know a lot, like Maria said. And I'm not afraid to say what I think, like Dad said. I'm kind and loving, like Mom said. And Ms.

Dobbins was right. Sometimes I have great ideas."
She lay down next to the sleepy pup. "I'm a mix,
just like you."

Muttley squirmed closer to her, sighed content-
edly, and licked her cheek.

I love you just the way you are.

"I love you, too, Muttley," said Lizzie. "And I
hope my article convinces Jimmy's mom that you
are a very special dog."

Later that night, Lizzie was sound asleep when
she heard Muttley barking. "Oh, no." She sat up
in her bed. "Not again."

"Nope," she heard her mother say. "It's just
me." And then Lizzie saw her standing in the
doorway.

"Mom!" Lizzie jumped out of bed and ran to hug
her mother. "You came home early!"

Mom laughed and squeezed Lizzie tight. "I drove
all day. Your aunt Julie is feeling much better,

and when I heard about all the excitement here, I couldn't stand to be away from all of you for another minute," she said softly. "Now, go back to bed before your brothers wake up. It's very late. I'll see you in the morning." She kissed the top of Lizzie's head.

Lizzie went back to her bed to lie down, certain that she was too wound up to sleep. But Muttley padded in and curled in a ball at the bottom of her bed, and his soft sleepy snores were like a lullaby.

CHAPTER TEN

"'Local shelter mutt is purebred hero.'" Mom read the headline aloud. "What's this?" She took a closer look at the article. "By special reporter Lizzie Peterson." She leaned back in her seat and beamed at Lizzie. "Well!"

"What?" asked Charles. "You wrote an article?"

Lizzie nodded. "It's about what Muttley did," she said. She had woken up early that morning and tiptoed out to the driveway to get the paper, her heart racing with excitement. She'd read the article five times before she folded the paper and set it at her mom's place at the kitchen table.

"Yay, Muttley!" The Bean waved his toast, dripping jelly onto the floor. Buddy and Muttley raced to lick it up.

Everybody was in a great mood. It was wonderful to have Mom back home. Charles kept jumping up from his seat to hug her, and the Bean would not get out of her lap, and Dad refilled her coffee cup every time she took a sip. It made Lizzie happy to look across the table and see Mom there. She beamed at her mother. Even without the newspaper article, this would have been a perfect, perfect morning.

Mom was still staring at the newspaper. "This is amazing, sweetie. How did you talk Mr. Baker into it?"

Lizzie shrugged. "Ms. Dobbins did the convincing," she said.

Mom started to read out loud. "'Muttley, a mixed-breed puppy from the Caring Paws animal shelter, became a hero when he smelled smoke in the middle of the night. The scrappy pup raced upstairs, barking, when a pot of chili left on the stove began to burn.'" Mom lowered the paper and smiled over it at Lizzie. "Excellent lead, Lizzie," she said.

Lizzie grinned. "Keep reading, keep reading!" she said.

Mom read through the article to the end. "'Muttley will be honored at a special ceremony on Sunday at eleven-thirty a.m. on the steps of the town hall,'" she read. "'The public is invited to attend.'"

Dad checked his watch. "Eleven-thirty?" he asked. "We'd better get a move on if we want to get the guest of honor there on time." He got up and started to clear the table.

Muttley snoozed on the floor near Mom's chair. She reached down to ruffle his floppy ears. "What a good puppy," she said. "What a hero."

Muttley licked her hand sleepily.

Me? A hero? Well, if you say so.

"So you're not mad that we haven't found him a home yet?" Lizzie asked.

"Are you kidding?" Mom said. "He saved your

lives. I love this puppy. This puppy deserves a medal!"

"I bet Muttley will have a forever home by the end of the day," said Dad. "When people hear about what he did, they'll be lining up to adopt him."

Lizzie hoped that Jimmy's mom would be first in line. "And some of the other dogs at Caring Paws might find forever homes, too" — Lizzie held up her crossed fingers — "once some of that publicity starts to work."

Everybody bustled around, getting ready to go. At the last minute, the phone rang. Dad picked it up. "Hello?" he said. A moment later, he waved to Mom. "You go ahead," he said. "I'll follow you in the other car." Then he went back to the phone call.

When the rest of the Petersons and Muttley arrived at the town hall, a small crowd had already begun to gather. Ms. Dobbins was there, handing out flyers about some of the other dogs available for adoption at Caring Paws. Lizzie waved at her.

Then she spotted Jimmy. His mom stood behind him, hands on his shoulders. Lizzie ran over to say hello.

"I made something for Muttley," Jimmy said. He dug in his jacket pocket and pulled out a medal on a wide red ribbon. It was made out of cardboard covered with tinfoil. "HERO," it said in big letters across the front.

"Wow," Lizzie said. "My mom just said that Muttley deserves a medal, but I never thought of making one. That's cool."

Jimmy knelt down to put the medal around Muttley's neck. Then he gave Muttley a long hug and a kiss on the nose. Lizzie felt a lump in her throat as she watched Jimmy whisper into Muttley's ear. Muttley's tail swished back and forth as he licked Jimmy's cheek. How could Jimmy's mom resist when she saw how much Jimmy and Muttley loved each other? Maybe by the time the ceremony was over, she would decide to adopt Muttley.

"Hey, Lizzie," someone said, and Lizzie turned to see Daphne and Brianna. "That was a pretty cool article in the paper," said Daphne.

Lizzie could tell it wasn't easy for Daphne to give compliments. "Thanks," she said. Now maybe it was time to for her to give Daphne a compliment. After all, even if she was a pain, she had been really good with the animals at Caring Paws. Daphne was a mix, too. "Who knows?" Lizzie said. "If we didn't have Muttley, maybe our house would have burned down. And it was your idea that we should foster him. So I guess we owe you a big thank-you."

Daphne smiled. "By the way, I might be able to come to Caring Paws this week," she said.

"Me, too," said Brianna. "Do you think Ms. Dobbins will still need us?"

"Definitely," said Lizzie. "I know she'd be really happy to have you back."

Daphne and Brianna knelt to give Muttley

some hugs, and Lizzie and Jimmy smiled at each other.

Then Chief Olson walked to the microphone at the top of the steps and waved at the crowd for attention. "Welcome, everybody," he said. "Thank you for coming down to honor a hometown hero." He held up a certificate. "I'd like to present this award to Muttley, a brave and caring temporary member of the Peterson family." Chief Olson told the story of how Muttley had smelled smoke and woken everyone up before things could get serious. Then he beckoned to Lizzie. "Lizzie, would you bring Muttley on up?"

Lizzie looked down at Muttley, who was draped over one of her sneakers, settled in for a short nap. "Psst, Muttley," she said. "Wake up! It's time for your award." Muttley stretched out all four legs and groaned.

Do I have to?

Then Muttley rose to his feet and let Lizzie lead him up the stairs. His medal glinted in the sun as he sat next to Chief Olson. A photographer stepped forward and took pictures as Chief Olson handed the certificate to Lizzie. As she took it, she began to cry a little and had to wipe her eyes with her other hand. She was so proud of Muttley.

"Thank you," she said as the crowd applauded. She caught Ms. Dobbins's eye and added, "And don't forget: there are lots of other great dogs at Caring Paws, and they're all looking for homes." Lizzie bent to show the certificate to Muttley.

When she straightened, she saw Dad making his way up the stairs, along with a man who looked familiar to Lizzie. "We have an announcement to add." Dad leaned over to speak into the microphone. "This is Mark, who met Muttley the night he became a hero. Mark is an EMT from Springfield. He called me this morning to say that he's decided to adopt Muttley and give him a great forever home."

That's where Lizzie knew him from! It was the EMT guy who had said he might adopt Muttley. And now he had been the first to speak up — before Jimmy's mother had the chance to change her mind and adopt Muttley. Lizzie felt her stomach sink. She turned to find Jimmy's face in the crowd. She could hardly stand to look. He must be disappointed. But there was Jimmy, grinning as he galloped up the steps two at a time. "Dad!" he said. "Really? You mean it?" He threw his arms around Mark.

Lizzie's head was spinning. Her own dad came over to put his arm around her. "Isn't it great?" he whispered. "It turns out that Mark is Jimmy's dad. The guys on his crew want Muttley to be their firehouse mascot. Mark called just before we left to say that he had made up his mind, and I was so happy to tell him how much Muttley and Jimmy already love each other."

"Can you believe it, Lizzie?" Now Jimmy was on his knees with his arms around Muttley. "Muttley's going to be my very own dog."

Once again, Lizzie had to wipe her eyes. There was no question in her mind: Muttley had found the perfect forever home.

PUPPY TIPS

Muttley might seem lazy, but he is also alert and caring. Like all dogs, he has his own personality. Some of a dog's personality comes from his breed: Most German shepherds like to take care of their people, most Labs are goofy and friendly, many terriers can be bossy.

But even within breeds, every dog is different — just like people are different! Some dogs have a great sense of humor, while others are very serious. Some like to play, some like to sleep. Some dogs are friendly, some are shy.

We also help to create our dogs' personalities, by encouraging certain behaviors and discouraging others. If you reward your dog when he is acting friendly, he will want to act friendly more often.

Think about your own dog's personality. What parts come from his breed, what parts come from the way you treat him, and what parts are just special to him?

DEAR READER,

The character of Muttley is based on one of my best dog friends, a sweet, funny mutt named Barley, who lives next door. Barley is part German shepherd and part Walker hound, just like Muttley. He loves to sleep and he can be cranky if you try to wake him up from his nap. But he also loves to play, especially with his dog sister Ursa, who is also a mutt (part Lab, part Samoyed). Barley loves to kiss me — but he does not like to be kissed! He loves treats and he takes them very gently from my hand. He loves to chase squirrels, take long walks in the woods, and ride in the car. Barley may not be a hero like Muttley, but he has a special, very lovable personality, and I am glad he is my friend.

Yours from the Puppy Place,
Ellen Miles

P.S. For another smart puppy, check out SHADOW!

ABOUT THE AUTHOR

Ellen Miles likes to write about the different personalities of dogs. She is the author of more than 30 books, including the Puppy Place and Taylor-Made Tales series as well as *The Pied Piper* and other Scholastic Classics. Ellen loves to be outdoors every day, walking, biking, skiing, or swimming, depending on the season. She also loves to read, cook, explore her beautiful state, and hang out with friends and family. She lives in Vermont.

If you love animals, be sure to read all the adorable stories in the Puppy Place series!

SOPHIE

SOPHIE the AWESOME
by Lara Bergen
SCHOLASTIC

Sophie knows she's special — now she just needs the perfect name to show it!

SOPHIE the HERO
by Lara Bergen
SCHOLASTIC

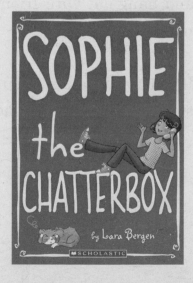

SOPHIE the CHATTERBOX
by Lara Bergen
SCHOLASTIC